BOOKWORMS CLUB

Bronze

STORIES FOR READING CIRCLES
Stage 1 (400 headwords)
Stage 2 (700 headwords)

The seven short stories in this book come from different volumes in the Oxford Bookworms Library. There are five stories at Stage 1 and two stories at Stage 2. All have been specially chosen for Reading Circles.

The stories are all very different. There are stories set in Turkey, in Finland, in New York, and in England. There are modern stories, about sisters and their boyfriends, and about secret agents and drug companies. There are stories about life in the last century, stories about city life and country life. Different times and different places, but we see that people's hopes and dreams do not change – a child wanting a toy, boys wanting to be men, young women wanting to get married. Love and hate, laughter and sadness can all be found in these stories.

OXFORD BOOKWORMS LIBRARY
Series Editor: Jennifer Bassett
Founder Editor: Tricia Hedge

BOOKWORMS CLUB
Bronze

STORIES FOR READING CIRCLES

Editor:
Mark Furr

OXFORD UNIVERSITY PRESS

Great Clarendon Street, Oxford OX2 6DP

Oxford University Press is a department of the University of Oxford.
It furthers the University's objective of excellence in research, scholarship,
and education by publishing worldwide in

Oxford New York

Auckland Cape Town Dar es Salaam Hong Kong Karachi
Kuala Lumpur Madrid Melbourne Mexico City Nairobi
New Delhi Shanghai Taipei Toronto

With offices in

Argentina Austria Brazil Chile Czech Republic France Greece
Guatemala Hungary Italy Japan Poland Portugal Singapore
South Korea Switzerland Thailand Turkey Ukraine Vietnam

OXFORD and OXFORD ENGLISH are registered trade marks of
Oxford University Press in the UK and in certain other countries

8 10 9 7

ISBN 978 0 19 472000 7

Printed in Hong Kong

CONTENTS

SOURCE OF STORIES

The seven stories in this book were originally published in different volumes in the OXFORD BOOKWORMS LIBRARY. They appeared in the following titles:

The Horse of Death
Sait Faik, from *The Meaning of Gifts: Stories from Turkey*
Translated from Turkish into English by Sylvia Seden
Retold for Oxford Bookworms by Jennifer Bassett

The Little Hunters at the Lake
Yalvac Ural, from *The Meaning of Gifts: Stories from Turkey*
Translated from Turkish into English by Sema Ozkaya
Retold for Oxford Bookworms by Jennifer Bassett

Mr Harris and the Night Train
Jennifer Bassett, from *One-Way Ticket: Short Stories*

Sister Love
John Escott, from *Sister Love and Other Crime Stories*

Omega File 349: London, England
Jennifer Bassett, from *The Omega Files: Short Stories*

Tildy's Moment
O. Henry, from *New Yorkers*
Retold by Diane Mowat

Andrew, Jane, the Parson, and the Fox
Thomas Hardy, from *Tales from Longpuddle*
Retold by Jennifer Bassett

Welcome to Reading Circles

Reading Circles are small groups of students who meet in the classroom to talk about stories. Each student has a special role, and usually there are six roles in the Circle:

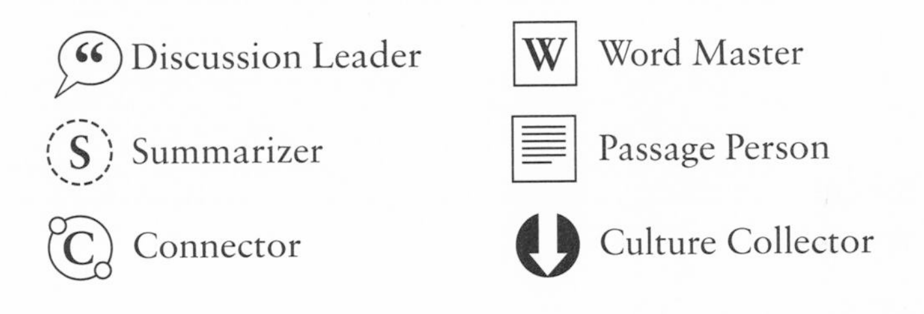

Each role has a role sheet with notes and questions which will help you prepare for your Reading Circle discussions in the classroom. You can read more about the roles and the role sheets on pages 77 to 83 at the back of this book.

The stories in this book have been specially chosen for Reading Circles. They have many different themes, and students everywhere enjoy reading them and talking about them in their Circle. Everybody's ideas are important; there are no 'right' or 'wrong' answers when you are talking about stories.

Enjoy the reading, enjoy the talking – and discover the magic of Reading Circles . . .

Mark Furr
Hawaii, May 2006

The Horse of Death

~

Little Unal must stay in bed because he has measles. But the sun is shining, and it is a beautiful day. From his bedroom window he can see the toy shop across the road, and he stands at the window, looking out and thinking. There are so many toys in that shop window! Big and small, in all colours! But the most wonderful toy is a horse, a big black horse with a long tail and lights in its eyes.

More than anything in the world, Unal wants to ride that horse . . .

SAIT FAIK

The Horse of Death

Retold by Jennifer Bassett

Little Unal was ill. He had the measles and so he was in bed. But he was bored. 'What can I do?' he thought. 'The doctor says I can't go out, but the sun is shining and it's a beautiful day!'

That morning, when his mother left the house, she said to Unal's grandmother, 'The sun is shining but it's very cold. Be careful with Unal, Mother. We don't want him to catch cold.'

From his window Unal could look out at the street. And when his grandmother came into his room, Unal was at the window, wearing only his pyjamas.

'What did your mother tell you?' said his grandmother. 'And what did the doctor say? Do you want to catch cold, and die, like your grandfather? Come now, go back to bed.'

'Grandma, what beautiful weather! And I'm not ill. I haven't got a fever.'

'No, thank God, you haven't got a fever. But it's easy to catch cold. And then those red spots on your face are going to go inside you.'

'Good!' said Unal.

'No, it's not good. Those red spots can kill you, so you must be careful. Come now, get back into bed.'

Unal got back into bed, and his grandmother went back to the kitchen.

Unal's father was dead. He died before Unal was born. Now his grandfather was dead too, so Unal had nobody to call 'father'. His mother worked as a cleaning woman in the government offices in the town. It was not a good job and the family did not have much money.

During that day, Unal was sometimes in bed, and sometimes at the window. When his grandmother came into the room, Unal got back into bed. When she left, he ran back to the window.

Across the street there was a toy shop, and Unal watched it from his window. Today was New Year's Day and there were bright lights in the toy shop window. What wonderful toys there were – animals and cars, big and small, in all colours! But the most wonderful thing was a black horse. Oh, Unal wanted that horse so much! When you pulled the reins, there were lights in the horse's eyes. It had a long tail and a beautiful brown mane.

Unal stood at the window, watching, thinking, imagining. 'Now I'm riding that black horse,' he said to himself. 'I'm not ill. There's nothing wrong with me – of course there isn't. When I'm riding the black horse, I don't get cold, I'm not ill, and there are no red spots on my face.'

Then he heard his grandmother at the door, and he ran back to bed.

When his grandmother came in, she said, 'That's a good boy, Unal! Stay in bed, and you can have something nice for dinner tonight. Now, I've still got a lot of work to do in the kitchen. Remember – don't get out of bed.' She went out and closed the door.

It was now dark and all the lights of the toy shop window shone brightly across the street. Unal got up and dressed, then left his room quietly. He couldn't find his shoes, but he found some old shoes of his grandmother's and put those on. He ran out into the street, and across to the toy shop.

There were a lot of women in the shop, with their children. Everybody bought toys for their children on New Year's Day. Unal didn't have any toys, but he didn't want them. He wanted that black horse. He wanted to ride it just one time. The shopkeeper was busy, everybody was busy. Nobody looked at a small eight-year-old boy.

Unal went in and walked around the shop, looking at things. Then he hid behind some big boxes, and waited.

Some time later, all the lights went out and the shopkeeper closed the doors and went away. The street lights outside shone into the shop. Unal went to the shop window and slowly opened the big glass door. Then he got into the window and climbed on to the back of the black horse. He pulled the reins, then looked at the horse's head. Yes, there were lights, bright shining lights, in the horse's eyes.

Unal began to ride. 'I can see snow on the ground all around me,' he said to himself. 'I can see clouds in the sky above, and silvery lights from the moon. Everything is so bright, so cold. I feel I am swimming in the sea, but the water is as cold as ice.'

He and the horse rode on. Then Unal began to feel warm again. Far away there was a light – the colour of Unal's blond hair. The horse rode on towards the yellow light.

It was the sun. Now Unal began to burn – his hair, his hands, everything was on fire. The black horse, too, burned like fire.

Then everything changed again. Unal felt strange, empty – first he was in deep water, then he was in the sky. He was not hot, or cold; he did not feel anything. He and his horse began to go faster – faster and faster . . .

∞

When Unal's grandmother next went to his room, Unal wasn't there. His grandmother was very afraid. She looked for him in the house, in the street, and she asked everybody, 'Where is Unal?'

But nobody knew. Other families in the street came to help, and people ran in and out of the house all night. Then, when morning arrived, a man came to the women in front of Unal's house.

'Look,' he said. 'Look there – in the window of the toy shop.'

Everybody ran to look. They saw a small boy on the back of the black horse, with a smile on his face. But he was dead, cold and dead.

They broke the shop window and tried to take Unal off the horse, but they could not move him. Unal belonged to the black horse now. He could not stop riding, riding, riding . . .

They took him home, still on the horse. His grandmother looked and looked at the child's blue face.

'Ah, Unal!' she said. 'What did the doctor tell you? Those red spots can kill people when they catch cold.'

Then a woman from the next house spoke. 'When somebody wants to ride the black horse of death, nobody can stop him.'

They buried Unal and the black horse together in the cold ground.

Word Focus

Match each word with an appropriate meaning.

bury (*past tense* buried)	an illness when your body is too hot
buy (*past tense* bought)	sending out bright light
catch cold	small, sore red marks on your skin
fever	an illness when you get small red spots on the skin
hide	to put a dead person in the ground
measles	to give money to get something
shining	to get ill with a cold
spots	to be in a place where people cannot see you

Here is Unal's grandmother telling a friend the sad story of Unal's illness. Use six of the eight words above to complete what she says. (Use one word in each gap.)

'My grandson Unal was ill with the _____. He had red _____ all over his face. I was very worried about him, and told him to stay in bed. But it was a beautiful day and the sun was _____, and Unal didn't want to stay in bed. I know he often got out and stood at the window, looking out. I told him, "You must stay in bed or you will _____ _____. Then you will get a _____ and die like your grandfather." But later in the afternoon, when I went to look in his room again, Unal wasn't there. I looked everywhere for him. The next morning we found him on the back of the black horse in the window of the toy shop. He was dead, but he had a smile on his face. We _____ Unal and the horse together. I can never forget that terrible day . . .'

Story Focus

Match these halves of sentences to make a paragraph of nine sentences.

1 Unal had red spots on his face . . .
2 Unal's grandmother told him to stay in bed, . . .
3 At the window, Unal looked at the toy shop . . .
4 When Unal's grandmother went to work in the kitchen, . . .
5 Then he went out into the street . . .
6 He hid in the toy shop and waited . . .
7 Later, Unal's grandmother went into his room, . . .
8 The next morning, a man saw Unal on the black horse in the toy shop window, . . .
9 They buried Unal and the black horse together . . .

10 . . . because he wanted to see the black horse.
11 . . . but Unal wasn't there.
12 . . . but Unal sometimes ran to the window.
13 . . . and ran across to the toy shop.
14 . . . because he had the measles.
15 . . . Unal got up and dressed.
16 . . . because they could not take him off the horse.
17 . . . but Unal was dead.
18 . . . because he wanted to ride the black horse.

The Little Hunters at the Lake

~

Men use guns and dogs to hunt. And young boys often want to do the same things as their fathers. They want to call the dogs and go down to the lake, shoot ducks and cook them over a fire, just like the men.

Hikmet secretly borrows his father's big hunting gun, and he and his friends go down to the lake. They are excited, laughing, making big plans. They think they are hunters now, just like the men. But they are only boys, and still have a lot to learn . . .

YALVAC URAL

The Little Hunters at the Lake

Retold by Jennifer Bassett

The sky above the little lake was full of birds – small birds, big birds, birds of all colours. We sat in the rain by Hikmet's garden wall and watched them.

'Winter's coming,' I said to my three friends. 'The birds are beginning to leave and fly away to warm countries.'

Then a hunting dog came by. It stopped and smelled all of us, then went away.

'Is that Tekin's dog from the village?' asked Peker.

'Yes, it is,' said Hikmet. 'But what's it doing here in the rain?'

'Perhaps the hunters are coming out to the lake,' I said.

Then we saw them. There was Tekin, the driver Nuri, Halil, and two more men. They wore hunting clothes and carried guns. We all wanted to go with them. Peker spoke for all of us.

'I'd like to have a gun and be a hunter, too,' he said.

Then Hikmet got up and ran into his house. He came back with something in a bag under his arm.

'What is it?' we said, but we already knew.

Hikmet opened the bag and we looked at the long, beautiful gun.

'Hey, that's wonderful!'

'Of course it is!'

'How much is it?'

'Forty thousand.'

'Wow!'

'Your father's going to be angry.'

'Yes. But I can put the gun back before he comes home.'

'OK,' we all said, and began to walk to the lake. First Hikmet carried the gun, then me, then Peker, and then Muammer. We were all hunters now.

'We've got five bullets,' Hikmet said. 'So we can all shoot once. Then I can shoot a second time, with the fifth bullet, because I brought the gun.'

'And when we've got five dead birds, we can cook them and eat them,' said Peker.

At the lake we could see the hunters and hear the noise of their dogs. We, too, waited by the lake and watched. It rained, and stopped, then rained again. But there were no birds on the lake or in the sky – not one.

We waited, but then we began to think about Hikmet's angry father.

'Shall we go home now and put the gun back?' said Muammer.

Then, suddenly, we saw three ducks. They flew down to the ground not far from us. Hikmet stood up quietly and tried to shoot one of the ducks. He didn't hit it, of course, and the ducks flew away. But the gun made a very loud noise, and now the sky was full of thousands of birds!

During the day the birds hide around the lake, and the hunters wait for the evening before they begin to shoot. But we learned all this later.

Now the birds were afraid because of the noise. They all flew away and so the hunters had nothing to shoot.

The hunters began to chase us, shouting angrily. But we could run faster, and so we escaped. Soon we stopped, and began to talk and laugh.

'Where's our duck dinner, then?' said Muammer.

I laughed. 'Wait until tomorrow,' I said. 'Or the next day – when Hikmet can shoot!'

'Hunters don't always come home with lots of dead birds,' said Hikmet. 'Listen. The birdseller Ali shoots birds. And who does he sell them to?'

'To the hunters!' Peker said.

'Right!' Hikmet said. 'And why? Because people laugh at hunters when they come home with nothing. So the hunters go quietly to Ali, buy his dead birds, and then they can talk about all their exciting hunts!'

Suddenly I saw some birds in the sky. 'Be quiet,' I told my friends. I took the gun, put a bullet in it, and waited. When the birds were right above me, I shot. Two birds fell out of the sky and down to the ground. Shouting happily, we ran to the place. But just then, one of the birds flew back up from the ground, high into the sky. We were very surprised.

We soon found the other bird. It was big, with a long neck. Hikmet looked at it.

'It's dead,' he said.

'The second bird was only hurt, perhaps,' said Muammer.

We looked carefully at the dead bird, but we all felt a little afraid. Was it really dead? High in the sky above us, the second bird flew round and round in circles, giving long, sad cries.

We began to carry our dead bird home, and after a time the bird in the sky flew away.

'When are we going to eat this bird?' asked Muammer.

'Tomorrow,' said Hikmet.

'Who's going to cook it?'

'We are!'

'But we don't know how!'

'Let's go to the birdseller Ali and ask him.'

We put the gun back in Hikmet's house and ran to Ali's shop. There were a lot of dead birds in the shop, but our bird was different.

'Hello, boys,' Ali said. 'What can I do for you?'

'We shot a bird,' we said, 'but what is it, and how do we cook it?'

Ali smiled. 'Well, you boys are better hunters than the men!'

We put the bag with our bird on Ali's table and opened it. Ali stopped smiling. He quickly put the bird back into the bag, and for a minute or two he said nothing.

Then he said, 'Look, children, you don't understand. You can't eat this bird! Take it back, and bury it in the ground.'

We looked at him with our mouths open in surprise.

Then Ali asked, 'Was his mate with him there?'

'There was another bird, but it flew away,' said Hikmet.

'Good,' said Ali, and smiled. He began to say something, but stopped.

'Did we really do something terrible?' asked Hikmet.

'Listen,' said Ali. 'These birds are called cranes – you know, the famous "crane" in our songs. Hunters never shoot them because they are the "symbols of love".'

We did not understand this, but we understood the words 'take it back and bury it'. It was nearly dark, but we went back to the lake and found the right place. Then we dug a hole and buried our crane there. I think we all cried a little, because we felt so sad.

After that day we never talked about hunting. We had a long cold winter that year. In the spring, we began to play outside again, but there was still some snow on the ground.

'Let's go and look at our crane's grave,' Hikmet said one day.

We all wanted to do this, but Hikmet was the first to say the words. We walked quietly to the lake, then Peker said, 'I asked Dad about "symbols of love" one day.'

'And what does it mean?' asked Muammer.

'It means that cranes know how to love. Their love is the best and the strongest in the world.'

There was still snow on our crane's grave, but we could see two snowdrops too. Snowdrops are always the first flowers of spring. Hikmet began to move the snow away from the top of the grave, but suddenly he stopped. There was something under the snow. Then we saw it.

It was our crane. It lay there on the ground, icy cold, on top of its grave. We felt very sad.

'Who took it out?' said Peker.

'Perhaps it was wild dogs,' answered Hikmet. 'And then they couldn't eat it because it was frozen.'

'Oh, why didn't we dig a deeper hole?' cried Muammer.

'We can do that now,' said Hikmet. 'God stopped the wild dogs from eating our crane, so now we must bury it deeper.'

Sadly, we began to dig. Soon the hole was open, but then we suddenly saw something, and stopped very quickly. There was *another* crane in the hole. We looked at it, and felt afraid. Nobody could speak.

Hikmet took our crane out. Then he put it on the ground and began to cry. We all cried too, but we did not know why.

Hikmet stood up. 'I was afraid of this,' he said, 'and I didn't want it to happen.'

We did not understand.

'Cranes, symbols of love, please forgive us,' Hikmet said quietly. Then he looked at us. 'Cranes are very loving birds,' he said, 'and the male and the female stay together all their lives. Cranes always live in warm places, but when a crane dies, its mate goes to a cold snowy place. Then it dies in the snow, and nobody can eat it. People do not eat birds that die in this way. And hunters never shoot cranes because they know all these things.'

Our hearts were very sad. We buried the two birds together in the hole and put snowdrops all over their grave. And after that day, every time we heard the word 'love', we thought about the cranes.

And we never forgot to go to the grave every spring.

One spring morning when I woke up, I saw a pair of cranes at my window. I ran to the window, but they flew away. Then I saw some snowdrops there. I took the flowers in my hand, held them to my face, and began to cry. Some minutes later, I heard someone at the door.

Hikmet was there, his eyes red from crying. There were snowdrops in his hand too.

'They forgive us,' Hikmet said. 'The cranes forgive us.'

WORD FOCUS

Use the clues below to help you complete this crossword with words from the story.

		1													
2															
						3									
		4											5		
											6				
						7					8				
									9						

ACROSS

2 Ali told the children to bury the dead bird in the _____.

3 Hikmet got his father's gun because the boys wanted to be _____ like the men.

4 The boys buried the birds together and put flowers on their _____.

6 The big bird with a long neck was a _____.

7 In Ali's shop, Hikmet asked Ali, 'Did we do something _____?'

9 Hunters never shoot cranes because they are a _____ of love.

DOWN

1 'Cranes, symbols of love, please _____ us,' Hikmet said quietly.

3 When the boys found the crane's dead mate, their _____ were very sad.

5 Cranes are loving birds and stay with their _____ all their lives.

8 Ali told the boys to _____ the dead bird.

Story Focus 1

In a story, the narrator is a character who tells the story. What do you think about the narrator of *The Little Hunters at the Lake*? Choose one of these adjectives for the first gaps, and then write as much as you like to finish the sentences.

afraid, excited, happy, pleased, right, sad, sorry, surprised, wrong

1 I think that the narrator was _____ because ________.
2 I think that the narrator was _____ to ________.
3 The narrator was _____ when ________.
4 When they found the second dead crane, the narrator was _____ because ________.
5 When the narrator found snowdrops at his window, he was _____ because ________.

Story Focus 2

Match these halves of sentences to make a paragraph of five sentences. Who do you think the narrator is here?

1 When I got home, . . .
2 I looked everywhere, . . .
3 Then I thought, 'Hikmet took the gun . . .
4 I was angry . . .
5 Finally, when Hikmet came home, . . .

6 . . . because he wants to be a hunter.'
7 . . . I locked the gun in a cabinet and told him to leave it alone.
8 . . . my gun was not in its usual place.
9 . . . but I could not find it.
10 . . . because guns are dangerous for young boys.

Mr Harris and the Night Train

~

A long journey on a train is like a holiday from your everyday life. You are in a closed world and you cannot leave it until the train stops. Sometimes people talk to you, and tell you all the secrets of their lives. Sometimes you see and hear very surprising things, very strange things, very frightening things . . .

Mr Harris always enjoys travelling by train. So he is a happy man when his train leaves Helsinki station to travel north through Finland during the night. There are not many people on the train, and Mr Harris is hoping for a nice quiet journey . . .

JENNIFER BASSETT

Mr Harris and the Night Train

Mr Harris liked trains. He was afraid of aeroplanes, and didn't like buses. But trains – they were big and noisy and exciting. When he was a boy of ten, he liked trains. Now he was a man of fifty, and he still liked trains.

So he was a happy man on the night of the 14th of September. He was on the night train from Helsinki to Oulu in Finland, and he had ten hours in front of him.

'I've got a book and my newspaper,' he thought. 'And there's a good restaurant on the train. And then I've got two weeks' holiday with my Finnish friends in Oulu.'

There weren't many people on the train, and nobody came into Mr Harris's carriage. He was happy about that. Most people on the train slept through the night, but Mr Harris liked to look out of the window, and to read and think.

After dinner in the restaurant Mr Harris came back to his carriage, and sat in his seat next to the window. For an hour or two he watched the trees and lakes of Finland out of the window. Then it began to get dark, so he opened his book and began to read.

At midnight the train stopped at the small station of Otava. Mr Harris looked out of the window, but he saw nobody. The train moved away from the station, into the black night again. Then the door of Mr Harris's carriage opened, and two people came in. A young man and a young woman.

The young woman was angry. She closed the door and shouted at the man: 'Carl! You can't do this to me!' The young man laughed loudly and sat down.

Mr Harris was a small, quiet man. He wore quiet clothes, and he had a quiet voice. He did not like noisy people and loud voices. So he was not pleased. 'Young people are always noisy,' he thought. 'Why can't they talk quietly?'

He put his book down and closed his eyes. But he could not sleep because the two young people didn't stop talking.

The young woman sat down and said in a quieter voice: 'Carl, you're my brother and I love you, but please listen to me. You can't take my diamond necklace. Give it back to me now. Please!'

Carl smiled. 'No, Elena,' he said. 'I'm going back to Russia soon, and I'm taking your diamonds with me.' He took off his hat and put it on the seat. 'Elena, listen. You have a rich husband, but *I* – I have no money. I have nothing! How can I live without money? You can't give me money, so I need your diamonds, little sister.'

Mr Harris looked at the young woman. She was small, with black hair and dark eyes. Her face was white and afraid. Mr Harris began to feel sorry for Elena. She and her brother didn't look at him once. 'Can't they see me?' he thought.

'Carl,' Elena said. Her voice was very quiet now, and

Mr Harris listened carefully. 'You came to dinner at our house tonight, and you went to my room and took my diamond necklace. How could you do that to me? My husband gave the diamonds to me. They were his mother's diamonds before that. He's going to be very, very angry – and I'm afraid of him.'

Her brother laughed. He put his hand in his pocket, then took it out again and opened it slowly. The diamond necklace in his hand was very beautiful. Mr Harris stared at it. For a minute or two nobody moved and it was quiet in the carriage. There was only the noise of the train, and it went quickly on through the dark cold night.

Mr Harris opened his book again, but he didn't read it. He watched Carl's face, with its hungry eyes and its cold smile.

'What beautiful, beautiful diamonds!' Carl said. 'I can get a lot of money for these.'

'Give them back to me, Carl,' Elena whispered. 'My husband's going to kill me. You're my brother . . . Please help me. Please!'

Carl laughed again, and Mr Harris wanted to hit him. 'Go home, little sister,' Carl said. 'I'm not going to give the diamonds back to you. Go home to your angry husband.'

Suddenly there was a knife in the young woman's hand. A long, bright knife. Mr Harris watched with his mouth open. He couldn't speak or move.

'Give the diamonds back to me!' Elena cried. 'Or I'm going to kill you!' Her hand on the knife was white.

Carl laughed and laughed. 'What a sister!' he said. 'What a kind, sweet sister! No, they're my diamonds now. Put your knife away, little sister.'

But the knife in the white hand moved quickly: up, then down. There was a long, terrible cry, and Carl's body fell slowly on to the seat. The colour of the seat began to change to red, and the diamond necklace fell from Carl's hand on to the floor.

Elena's face was white. 'Oh no!' she whispered. 'Carl! Come back . . . come back! I didn't want to kill you!' But Carl didn't answer, and the red blood ran slowly over the floor. Elena put her head in her hands, and again in the carriage there was a long, terrible cry.

Mr Harris's face was white too. He opened his mouth, but he couldn't speak. He stood up, and carefully moved to the door. The young woman was quiet now. She didn't move or look up at Mr Harris.

In the corridor, Mr Harris ran. The guard was at the back of the train and Mr Harris got there in half a minute.

'Quickly!' Mr Harris said. 'Come quickly! An accident . . . a young woman . . . oh dear! Her brother is . . . is dead!'

The guard ran with Mr Harris back to the carriage. Mr Harris opened the door and they went inside.

There was no dead body of a young man. There was no young woman . . . no blood, no knife, no diamond necklace. Only Mr Harris's bags and his hat and coat.

The guard looked at Mr Harris, and Mr Harris looked at him.

'But . . .' Mr Harris began. 'But they were here! I saw them! She . . . the young woman . . . She had a knife and she . . . she killed her brother.'

'A knife, you say?' the guard asked.

'Yes,' Mr Harris said quickly. 'A long knife, and her brother took her diamonds, so she—'

'Ah! Diamonds!' the guard said. 'Was the young woman's name Elena?' he asked.

'Yes, it was!' Mr Harris said. 'How do you know that? Do you . . . Do you know her?'

'Yes – and no,' the guard said slowly. He thought for a minute, then looked at Mr Harris. 'Elena di Saronelli,' he said. 'She had dark eyes and black hair. Very beautiful. She was half-Italian, half-Finnish. Her brother was a half-brother. They had the same father, but *his* mother was Russian, I think.'

'Was? Had?' Mr Harris stared at the guard. 'But she . . . Elena . . . she's alive! And where is she?'

'Oh no,' said the guard. 'Elena di Saronelli died about eighty years ago. After she killed her brother with a knife, she jumped off the train, and died at once. It was near here, I think.' He looked out of the window, into the night. Mr Harris's face was very white again. 'Eighty years ago!' he whispered. 'What are you saying? Were she and her brother . . . But I saw them!'

'Yes, that's right,' the guard said. 'You saw them, but they're not alive. They're ghosts. They often come on the night train at this time in September. *I* never see them, but somebody saw them last year. A man and his wife. They were very unhappy about it. But what can I do? I can't stop Elena and Carl coming on the train.'

The guard looked at Mr Harris's white face. 'You need a drink,' he said. 'Come and have a vodka with me.'

Mr Harris didn't usually drink vodka, but he felt afraid. When he closed his eyes, he could see again Elena's long knife and could hear her terrible cry. So he went with the guard to the back of the train.

After the vodka, Mr Harris felt better. He didn't want to sleep, and the guard was happy to talk. So Mr Harris stayed with the guard and didn't go back to his carriage.

'Yes,' the guard said, 'it's a famous story. I don't remember it all. It happened a long time ago, of course. Elena's father was a famous man here in Finland. He was very rich once, but he had three or four wives and about eight children. And he liked the good things of life. So there wasn't much money for the children. Carl, the oldest son, was a bad man, people say. He wanted an easy life, and money in his hand all the time.'

The train hurried on to Oulu through the black night, and the guard drank some more vodka. 'Now, Elena,' he said. 'She didn't have an easy life with those three difficult men – her father, her brother, her husband. One year she visited her mother's family in Italy, and there she met her husband, di Saronelli. He was rich, but he wasn't a kind man. They came back to Finland, and Carl often visited their house. He wanted money from his sister's rich husband. Elena loved her brother, and gave him some money. But di Saronelli didn't like Carl and was angry with Elena. He stopped giving her money, and after that . . . well, you know the story now.'

'Yes,' Mr Harris said. 'Poor, unhappy Elena.'

Mr Harris stayed with his friends in Oulu for two weeks. They were quiet weeks, and Mr Harris had a good holiday. But he took the bus back to Helsinki. The bus was slow, and there were a lot of people on it, but Mr Harris was very happy. He didn't want to take the night train across Finland again.

WORD FOCUS

Match each word with an appropriate meaning. Then use nine of the twelve words to complete Mr Harris's postcard to a friend. (Use one word in each gap.) You will also need a tenth word, which is not in the list.

blood	a 'chair' on a train
bright	to speak very, very quietly
carriage	to move suddenly from a high place to a low place
corridor	a dead person that living people think they can see
diamond	a man who works on a train
fall (*past tense* **fell**)	full of light; shining strongly
ghost	the red liquid in a person's body
guard	very bad; making you afraid or unhappy
necklace	a 'room' on a train
seat	a beautiful, very expensive, bright stone
terrible	something beautiful that women wear round the neck
whisper	the long, narrow place on a train with doors to the carriages

Last night I saw two _____s! They came into my _____ on the train at midnight – a brother and a sister. The brother had his sister's _____ _____ *(two words)* in his pocket, and the young woman wanted it back. She was angry and afraid, and in the end she killed her brother with a knife. There was _____ all over the _____ and the floor. It was _____! I ran down the _____ to the back of the train and spoke to the _____. He told me that it all happened eighty years ago! I'm coming back to Helsinki by _____. Best wishes, Joseph Harris

Story Focus

Here are three short passages from the story. Read them and answer the questions.

> 'He's going to be very, very angry – and I'm afraid of him.'

1 Who said these words in the story, and to whom?
2 Who is the speaker talking about?
3 Why do you think the speaker is afraid?

> Mr Harris's face was white too. He opened his mouth, but he couldn't speak.

4 Why was Mr Harris's face white?
5 Another person in the carriage had a white face too. Who was it? Why was their face white?
6 Mr Harris couldn't speak, but perhaps he wanted to. What do you think he wanted to say?

> 'Eighty years ago! What are you saying? Were she and her brother . . . But I saw them!'

7 Who says these words in the story, and to whom?
8 Who are they talking about?
9 What is the speaker beginning to understand?

Sister Love

~

Some sisters have special feelings for each other. They are best friends, they help each other, they talk about their work and their boyfriends, their hopes and their dreams. Other sisters are not so friendly. Perhaps they have different interests; perhaps they just don't like each other.

Marcia and Karin are sisters. Karin is younger, beautiful, and she has many boyfriends. But Marcia is not beautiful, and she doesn't meet many men – until one Sunday when she meets Howard at church and brings him home to meet her family . . .

JOHN ESCOTT

Sister Love

Marcia met Howard Collins at church. Marcia was thirty-five years old, Howard was forty-one. Howard lived with his mother in a small house on the south side of the town. Marcia lived with her sister and father in an apartment, three streets away.

Marcia did not work. Her father, George Grant, was ill and never left the apartment. He stayed in bed most of the time and always needed somebody with him. So Marcia stayed at home with her father, and only went out when her sister Karin was in the house.

The two sisters were very different. Marcia was short with a small round face and short black hair. Karin was ten years younger. She was tall, had long brown hair, and good legs, and a suntan all through the summer. People often said to Marcia, 'Your sister is very beautiful.' There were always lots of men ready to take Karin out to dinner or to the cinema. But Marcia stayed at home.

Karin worked in a shop in the town. When she was at home, she liked to sit up on the roof garden of their apartment building.

It was one Sunday in May when Marcia came home with Howard the first time. She took him to see her father.

George Grant was in bed. He had grey hair and a grey

face. Sometimes he read a book, but mostly he just sat in bed and watched television.

'This is Howard, father,' Marcia said. 'He works at the hospital, and we met at church. I told you about him last week. Do you remember?'

'No,' her father said. And he turned his face away, back to his television. He was not interested in new people or his daughters' friends.

Just then, Karin came into the room. She wore a white bikini and white shoes. She smiled at Howard.

'So you're Howard,' she said. 'My big sister has got a boyfriend at last!'

Howard's face went red and he looked down at his feet.

Karin laughed. 'Come on up to the roof garden and have some wine. The sun is wonderful this morning.'

'Oh, I . . .' Howard began.

Marcia looked angrily at her sister. But then she said, 'Yes, I must get father a drink. See you in a minute, Howard. Go up to the roof and talk to Karin.'

The sun was hot on the roof and Howard took off his coat. He looked around. There were three chairs, a sun umbrella, a sunbed, and a table with three glasses and a bottle of wine on it. There were tiles on the floor, and next to the little wall around the edge of the roof there were some flowers in boxes. This was the 'garden'.

'Very nice,' said Howard.

Karin smiled at him.

'We don't see many good-looking men up here,' she said. 'Sit down and have a drink.'

Howard's face went red again. He gave a shy little laugh. 'Oh, er . . . thank you,' he said. He tried not to look at Karin's long suntanned legs, but it was not easy.

'I come up here all the time when it's sunny,' Karin said. She began to put suntan oil on her arms and legs.

Howard watched.

Then Marcia arrived, and the three of them sat in the sun and drank wine. Marcia looked at Howard with love in her eyes. She did not look at Karin.

Karin watched them. Her eyes went from her sister, to Howard, and back again to her sister. She smiled.

It was not a nice smile.

∞

Every Sunday morning after that, Marcia brought Howard home for a glass of wine after church. Howard stopped his car in the street outside the apartment building, and Marcia said, 'Sound the horn, Howard. Tell Karin we're here, then she can get the wine ready.'

So Howard gave three little toots on his car horn. On sunny days Karin always came to the wall at the edge of the roof, and looked over to wave at them. Then she went to get the wine.

She always wore her bikini or a very short skirt. Marcia never wore short skirts or a bikini.

'My legs are too fat for bikinis,' she told Howard.

'Your legs are . . . very nice,' he said shyly.

One day in June Karin asked Howard, 'What time do you finish work, Howard?'

'About six o'clock,' he said.

'Could you bring me home after work?' Karin said. 'My shop's very near the hospital – you drive right past it. And you only live three streets away from us.'

'There's a very good bus,' said Marcia quickly. 'It stops outside our building.'

'But the bus is so slow!' Karin said. 'Please, Howard!'

Howard looked from one sister to the other. 'Oh, well . . . er, yes, all right then,' he said.

'Thank you!' Karin said, and gave him a quick kiss.

So every evening Howard drove Karin home. On the first Friday they were an hour late. When they arrived, Marcia was at the door of the apartment building.

'What happened?' she asked. 'Why are you so late?'

'There was an accident,' Karin said. 'Three cars, all across the road – on that hill by the cinema, you know. We couldn't get past, we couldn't go back. There were so many cars! Nobody could move!'

Howard said nothing.

∞

It was a long, hot summer that year. Marcia went to church every Sunday morning, and Karin stayed at home with their father. When it was sunny – and it often was – Karin went up to her sunbed on the roof.

When Marcia went up to the roof garden, she always sat under the umbrella. But Karin put on lots of suntan oil and sat in the sun in her bikini.

'The hot sun's not good for your body,' Marcia said.

Karin laughed. 'Howard likes my body.'

'No, he doesn't!' Marcia said angrily.

'Oh, he does!' Karin said. 'He's very shy with women, but he always looks at my body *very* carefully. He does it all the time. Perhaps he wants me to take off—'

'Stop it, Karin!' Marcia said. 'Don't say those things!'

Karin laughed. 'What's the matter, big sister? Are you afraid I'm going to take him from you?'

Marcia did not answer.

❧

The next Sunday, Howard phoned Marcia early in the morning.

'I – I don't feel very well,' he said. 'I'm not going to church today.'

'My love, I'm sorry,' Marcia said. 'Can I phone you when I get home?'

'Yes, of course,' he said.

'I can't phone before one o'clock,' Marcia said. 'I'm going to be late back because there's a meeting after church. Something about Africa, I think.'

'Oh yes, I remember,' Howard said.

But Marcia was wrong. There was no meeting after church that morning. It was the next Sunday. So she left church at the usual time and arrived home at a quarter to twelve.

First she went in to see her father, but he was asleep. Then she phoned Howard, but there was no answer.

'Perhaps he's sleeping,' she thought. 'And his mother doesn't want to answer the phone.'

She went to her room and put on a long summer skirt. Then she went up to the roof garden.

She put her hand on the door to the roof . . . and stopped. The door was half open and she could hear voices. There was someone with Karin.

A man. Howard. *Howard?*

Marcia listened.

'I feel bad about this,' Howard said. 'We must tell Marcia soon, Karin.'

'No!' Karin said quickly. She gave a little laugh. 'It's our secret, Howard. Only for a little longer. All right?'

'I – I don't like . . .' he began.

'But you do love *me*, Howard,' Karin said. 'Not Marcia? Say you love me. Please!'

Marcia suddenly felt cold.

'You . . . you know I do,' Howard answered. 'But—'

Karin kissed him. 'It's our little secret. Oh, is your car outside, my love? We don't want Marcia to see it.'

'I didn't bring my car,' Howard said. 'I walked here.'

'Good,' Karin said. 'But it's getting late. You must go, before she comes home.'

They kissed again. 'See you tomorrow, usual time, usual place,' said Karin. 'Now, go!'

Marcia moved quickly and quietly away from the roof door, and ran to her bedroom. She did not want Howard or Karin to see her.

She heard their voices. Then the front door of the apartment opened and closed. Howard was gone.

Marcia sat on her bed for an hour. 'Why, why, *why*?' she thought. '*Why* does she do it? I stay at home with an old man all the time. I can't go out to work, I can't make new friends, I can't meet new people. I go shopping once a week and I go to church once a week. That's all. And then I met Howard. When he said "I love you", I was so happy. And now . . . ?'

Karin had everything. Good looks, a job, friends. She was young, she was beautiful, she could have any man. So why Howard? Why, why, *why*?

'It's not because she wants *him*,' Marcia thought. 'It's because I love him. It's because she doesn't want me to be happy.'

But you do love me, Howard. Not Marcia?

You know I do.

Was it true? Did Howard love Karin and not her? No! He saw only the beautiful, suntanned body. He didn't *know* her.

'She's not going to have him . . .' Marcia thought.

Every evening that week, Howard drove Karin home after work. And every evening they got later and later.

The next Sunday, Marcia didn't go to church.

'I've got a bad head,' she told Karin. 'I just phoned Howard and told him, and he's coming here after church as usual. I'm going back to sleep for an hour or two.' And she went into her bedroom and shut the door.

Later in the morning, when Karin was with their father, Marcia went up to the roof garden. Karin's bottle of suntan oil was on the table, and Marcia smiled.

When Karin came up to the roof, Marcia was in her chair under the umbrella with a book in her hand.

'Oh, is your head better?' Karin asked.

'Yes, thanks,' Marcia said.

Karin wore her bikini, a new yellow one. She opened her bottle of suntan oil.

'Oh, there's not much here,' she said. 'I must get some more.' She began to put some oil on her legs.

Twenty minutes later, Howard stopped his car in the street below. Up on the roof, Karin and Marcia heard the usual three little toots on his car horn.

'He's here,' Karin said excitedly. 'Your man's here, big sister!' And she laughed.

Yes, Marcia thought. *My man, not yours, Karin.*

Karin jumped up from her sunbed. She ran to the wall at the edge of the roof to look down and wave to Howard. She had no shoes on, and at the wall her feet suddenly slipped away from under her.

'Aaagh!' she cried.

She fell forward, and put out her hands to grab the wall. But the top of the wall was slippery too. Her hands could not hold it, and slipped away, off the wall, over the edge. And her body went on too, over the edge of the wall, and down . . .

Down . . . down . . . down . . .

Before she hit the ground, she knew.

Slippery . . . suntan oil . . . Marcia . . .

Word Focus

Later that day, after the accident, Howard spoke to the police. Complete the passage with these words. (Use one word in each gap.)

apartment, bikini, church, edge, forward, horn, hospital, know, love, roof, sunbed, suntan, toots, wave, work

'Yes,
I know Karin and her sister Marcia very
well. Most Sundays I came to their _____ after church,
and had a glass of wine with them. We usually sat in their _____
garden. Karin liked the sun, you see. She always wore her _____ and lay
on her _____ in the sun. She had a wonderful _____. She's a very beautiful
woman. We met every day after _____, and I drove her home. I work at the
_____, you see, and Karin's shop was very near there. Yes, we are . . .
we were . . . it's very difficult. I go to church with Marcia every
Sunday, but I ____ Karin, and Marcia didn't _____
about it. I wanted to tell her, but . . .

Today, Marcia didn't go to _____ because
she had a bad head. But she wanted me to come for a
drink after church as usual. When I arrived, I gave three little
_____ on my car _____. I always did this, and Karin always came to
the _____ of the roof to look down and _____ to me. Today I saw her
at the edge, but suddenly she fell _____, and then came head first
over the little wall . . . and . . . and down to the ground. It was
so quick, so sudden. I couldn't do anything . . .'

Story Focus 1

What do you think about the people in this story? Was Marcia clever? Choose names from the list and complete these sentences in your own words. Make as many sentences as you can.

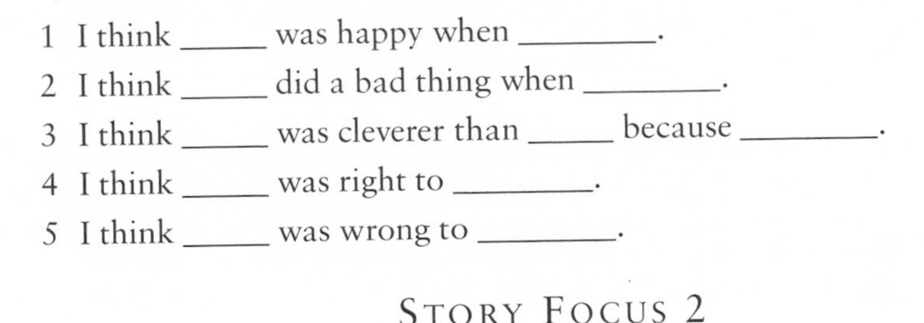

Marcia / Howard / Karin

1 I think _____ was happy when ________.
2 I think _____ did a bad thing when ________.
3 I think _____ was cleverer than _____ because ________.
4 I think _____ was right to ________.
5 I think _____ was wrong to ________.

Story Focus 2

Imagine that you are a policeman and you think that perhaps Karin's accident was not an accident at all. You listened to Howard, and now you want to talk to Marcia. You can ask her five questions about the accident, and about Howard. Which five questions will you ask her?

Omega File 349: London, England

~

The Omega Files don't get into the newspapers, and most people never hear about them. These files belong to the EDI – the European Department of Intelligence. There are secrets in the Omega Files. Big secrets, strange secrets.

A young man in London has a strange story to tell to Hawker and Jude, secret agents for the EDI. The young man's story is about a big drug company, but can it really be true? Who can believe a story like that? It's all there – in Omega File 349 . . .

JENNIFER BASSETT

Omega File 349: London, England

EDI
European Department of Intelligence

There were two of them. Hawker and Jude. They had no other names. Just Hawker and Jude. They were young, fast, and clever. They worked for EDI, in the European Government.

You know about the Americans' CIA and the Russians' KGB? Well, this was EDI – the European Department of Intelligence. Big secrets. Very strange secrets. The secrets of the Omega Files. They don't get into the newspapers, and most people never hear about them. Most people don't know anything about EDI.

In the early years Hawker and Jude travelled a lot. Brussels, Strasbourg, Rome, Delhi, Washington . . . North Africa, South America, Australia . . . No home, no family, just work. They worked for the top man in the Brussels office of EDI, and only for him. He was called Arla. Nobody knew his real name, or much about him. Some said he was Latvian; others said he was from another planet. He always gave the hard jobs to Hawker and Jude. The jobs with questions, but not many answers. The Omega Files.

When I met them, many years later, Hawker and Jude were about seventy years old. They lived very quietly, in a little white house on a Greek island. They went walking, swimming, fishing; they sat in the sun, and slept a lot.

At first, they didn't want to talk about their work.

'We can't,' said Jude. 'Our work was secret. It's all in the government files, and nobody can read them.'

'After thirty years,' I said, 'people can read all secret government files.'

'Not these files,' Hawker said. 'It's a hundred years before people can read the EDI files.'

I looked at them. 'But I don't need to read the files,' I said. 'I can get the stories from you.'

And I did. Here is one of them . . .

OMEGA FILE 349

LONDON, ENGLAND

'There's a young man in London called Johnny Cook,' Arla said. 'He's about eighteen. He doesn't have a home, but he goes clubbing nearly every night. Those all-night dance clubs for young people. Here's a photograph of him.'

He put the photograph on the table, and Jude and Hawker looked at it.

'And?' Hawker said.

'He wants to sell a story to a newspaper,' Arla said.

'Some story about a drug company. Find him. Talk to him. What's his story? I want to know.'

Jude and Hawker took an afternoon plane from Brussels to London, and then went to a hotel.

'What are you going to wear tonight?' said Jude. 'Not those old jeans, please!'

'What's wrong with them?' Hawker said. 'We're going clubbing, not out to dinner at the Ritz Hotel.'

'Well, wear a different shirt, then. That one's dirty.'

'You can wash it for me,' Hawker said.

'Get lost!' said Jude.

They had dinner, watched television for an hour or two, and then went out. It was a warm night, with a little rain now and then.

'London weather,' said Hawker.

They found a taxi with a young driver, and got in.

'Where to?' said the driver.

'We want to go clubbing,' Jude said. 'Where's the best place this week? Do you know?'

'Bruno's,' the driver said. 'Or Garcia's, down by the river. Everybody's going there this week.'

'OK, let's go!' said Hawker.

They went to Garcia's first, then moved on to Bruno's. They found Johnny Cook in a third club, called Monty's. It was two o'clock in the morning.

'That's him, all right,' Hawker said. 'Look at his ear.'

Johnny Cook was tall and thin, with long yellow hair and two black earrings in his left ear.

'Johnny! Johnny Cook!' shouted Jude suddenly. She ran and put her arms round Johnny Cook's neck. 'Hi, Johnny! You remember me – Jude. We met last week, at Garcia's. You remember? Oh, this is my friend Hawker.'

'Hi, Johnny. Good to meet you,' said Hawker.

'Hi,' said Johnny Cook. He looked at Jude. 'Did we meet at Garcia's?'

'Of course we did,' laughed Jude. 'I was with Sara and Patti and the others, remember?'

'Oh. Yeah,' said Johnny. 'I remember.' He looked around. 'Are they here tonight?'

'No, it's just me and Hawker tonight,' said Jude. 'Come on, let's dance.'

They danced for two hours. Then they left with about ten other people, and went across the river to a new club. The music there was louder and the dancing was very fast. After two more hours of dancing, Hawker was hot, tired, and thirsty.

'I'm getting old,' he said to Jude. 'Don't these people ever go to bed?'

'You're only twenty-five!' said Jude. 'That's not old. And you can't stop yet. He's getting very friendly now, and we can take him to breakfast soon.'

At seven o'clock the club closed, and Jude and Hawker took Johnny back to their hotel. Jude picked up the phone and asked for three big breakfasts in the room.

Hawker took his shoes off.

'Ah, that's better,' he said. He looked at Johnny. 'How often do you go clubbing, Johnny? And what do you do in the daytime?'

'Not a lot. Sleep, usually. I go clubbing most nights.'

'Where do you live?' Hawker asked.

'On the streets,' said Johnny. 'When I'm rich, I'm going to get a boat and live on that.'

'Rich?' Jude said. 'Oh yes, we all want to be rich!'

'But I *am* going to be rich,' Johnny said. 'I've got a good story, see?' He laughed. 'I'm going to sell it. A newspaper wants to give me 100,000 Euros for it. They gave me 1,000 last month, and I'm going to get the other 99,000 very soon.'

'Great!' said Jude. 'So what's the story then, Johnny? Have some more coffee, and tell us all about it.'

'Well, you know the Tyler Drug Company?' Johnny began. 'They make drugs and medicines.'

'Yes,' Hawker said. 'It's a very big European company. They've got offices in all the big cities.'

'Yeah, that's right,' Johnny said. 'Well, they're taking young people off the streets, and using them for tests.'

Jude laughed. 'Nobody's going to believe that!' she said. 'Drug companies use animals, not people, for their tests. Some new drugs can be very dangerous at first. Nobody wants people to die from a new medicine!'

'It's true!' Johnny said angrily. 'Think about it. All those young homeless people in London. They sleep every night along the Strand, and other streets. Nobody wants to know them, nobody asks questions about them. They've got no home, no family, nothing.'

'But they've got legs,' Hawker said. 'They can run away.'

'You don't understand,' said Johnny. 'Listen. I know, because I was there! I live on the streets, right? And late one night, along the Strand, they came and took me and some other people – a boy and two girls. They wanted to help us, they said. Hot food, nice beds, new clothes –

everything! They took us to this big house—'

'Where?' said Hawker.

'I'm not saying where,' said Johnny.

'And what happened?' asked Jude.

'They gave us food, and new clothes, and beds to sleep in, all right. But we couldn't get out of the house, and men in white coats watched us all the time. And they put drugs in our food.'

'How do you know that?' Hawker asked.

'I felt ill. My eyes went strange, and I couldn't see very well. And one of the girls – she got very ill one night. She screamed and screamed, and the men in white coats came. I was in the next room and I listened through the wall. "This is very strange," one of the men said. "She had 20 grams of Coplas in her dinner tonight. Was that too much, do you think?" "I don't know," said a second man. "We don't want to kill her. Let's try 20 grams again tomorrow, on this girl and on one of the boys. We can't stop this test now. We must get answers quickly." After that, they talked more quietly, and I couldn't hear. But I didn't eat any more food in that house, and the next night I got into an office downstairs and took some papers. Then I broke out of the house and ran away fast.'

'What papers?' said Hawker.

'Papers with Tyler Drug Company's name on them.'

'And where are those papers now?' asked Jude.

'That's my secret,' Johnny said. 'When the newspaper gives me the money, I'm going to tell them. But I'm not going to tell you.'

The next day Jude and Hawker flew back to Brussels and went to Arla's office. Arla listened to Johnny Cook's story, but he didn't say anything.

'So, what do we do now?' Jude said. 'Do we look for this big house and—'

Arla picked up his telephone. 'Come back in an hour,' he said. 'Get a coffee or something.'

An hour and three coffees later they went back.

'OK,' said Arla. 'You can forget all about this. Cook's story isn't true.'

Jude stared at him. 'Who told you that?' she said.

'I want to talk to Johnny Cook again,' Hawker said.

'You can't,' said Arla. 'He's dead.'

Hawker looked at Jude, and then back at Arla. 'He was alive yesterday,' said Hawker.

'Well, he isn't alive today. He came out of a club at three o'clock this morning and fell in the river Thames. When they got him out, he was dead.'

'But—' Jude began.

'Forget it, Jude. The file is closed.'

'And was that the end of it?' I asked, when Jude and Hawker finished telling the story.

'Yes,' said Hawker. 'Arla never spoke about it again.'

'And did you believe Johnny's story about the drug company?' I asked.

'Before a company can sell a new medicine to people,' said Hawker, 'there are years and years of tests. They do the tests on animals, of course. But they learn much more quickly from tests on people. There are lots of drug companies, and every company wants to be the first with a new medicine.'

'About five years later,' Jude said, 'the Tyler Drug Company began to sell a new drug, called Coplastin. It was a medicine to stop some kinds of cancer, and it worked. Everybody wanted it. The company made a lot of money – and so the government got a lot of money from the company in taxes. Governments like rich companies and big, fat taxes. They're not very interested in homeless young people sleeping on the streets.'

'So Johnny Cook's story was true,' I said. 'And he didn't fall into the river – somebody pushed him.'

'Of course they pushed him,' said Jude. 'Dead men can't talk, can they?'

Word Focus

Use the clues below and complete this crossword with words from the story.

Across

6 'They're using _____ young people off the streets for their tests.'

7 Governments get a lot of money in _____ from big companies.

9 Arla said Cook's story wasn't true, but Hawker and Jude _____ it.

10 There are years and years of tests before a new _____ comes out.

11 Johnny Cook had a story about a _____ _____. *(two words)*

12 A newspaper gave Johnny 1,000 _____ .

Down

1 Johnny did not _____ into the river – he was pushed.

2 Johnny's eyes went _____ because there were drugs in his food.

3 With new drugs, drug companies do _____ on animals.

4 Jude and Hawker worked for the European _____.

5 'We want to go _____,' Jude said to the taxi driver in London.

8 The Omega _____ were top secret.

Story Focus

Perhaps Johnny wrote some notes to use in his story for the newspaper. To read his secret notes, match these halves of sentences to make a paragraph of eleven sentences.

1 When I was sixteen years old, . . .
2 I hid on a train and went to London . . .
3 I met some new friends, . . .
4 One day, some men helped me, . . .
5 But one night, I felt ill, . . .
6 A girl in the next room also got very ill, . . .
7 I listened through the wall, . . .
8 The next night, I took some papers from the office, . . .
9 These papers were important . . .
10 Two days later, I phoned the newspaper . . .
11 Finally, the newspaper gave me 1,000 Euros, . . .

349

12 . . . and broke out of the house.
13 . . . and she screamed and screamed.
14 . . . and my eyes went strange.
15 . . . I left my home because my father was a very bad man.
16 . . . but I was always cold and had little food.
17 . . . because I wanted to get money for my story.
18 . . . and they're going to give me more money soon.
19 . . . because they had the drug company's name on them.
20 . . . and they took me to a house with hot food, a nice bed, and new clothes.
21 . . . because I knew there were many homeless young people there.
22 . . . and I learned that our food had drugs in it.

Tildy's Moment

~

Waitresses work hard, on their feet all day, running around the restaurant, but they meet a lot of people. Tildy and Aileen, waitresses at Bogle's Family Restaurant in New York, are always busy, but Aileen has more friends than Tildy. The men who come to eat their lunch at Bogle's are always watching Aileen, because Aileen is tall and beautiful, and poor Tildy is short and fat and not beautiful.

Tildy likes Aileen, and is happy that Aileen has lots of men friends. But sometimes, deep inside, Tildy wants a man to love her, too . . .

O. HENRY

Tildy's Moment

Retold by Diane Mowat

Bogle's Family Restaurant on Eighth Avenue is not a famous place, but if you need a large cheap meal, then Bogle's is the place for you. There are twelve tables in the room, six on each side. Bogle himself sits at the desk by the door and takes the money. There are also two waitresses and a Voice. The Voice comes from the kitchen.

At the time of my story, one of the waitresses was called Aileen. She was tall, beautiful and full of life. The name of the other waitress was Tildy. She was small, fat and was not beautiful.

Most of the people who came to eat at Bogle's were men, and they loved the beautiful Aileen. They were happy to wait a long time for their meals because they could look at her. Aileen knew how to hold a conversation with twelve people and work hard at the same time.

And all the men wanted to take Aileen dancing or give her presents. One gave her a gold ring and one gave her a little dog.

And poor Tildy?

In the busy, noisy restaurant men's eyes did not follow Tildy. Nobody laughed and talked with her. Nobody asked her to go dancing, and nobody gave her presents. She was a good waitress, but when she stood by the tables, the men looked round her to see Aileen.

But Tildy was happy to work with no thanks, she was happy to see the men with Aileen, she was happy to know that the men loved Aileen. She was Aileen's friend. But deep inside, she, too, wanted a man to love her.

Tildy listened to all Aileen's stories. One day Aileen came in with a black eye. A man hit her because she did not want to kiss him. 'How wonderful to have a black eye for love!' Tildy thought.

One of the men who came to Bogle's was a young man called Mr Seeders. He was a small, thin man, and he worked in an office. He knew that Aileen was not interested in him, so he sat at one of Tildy's tables, said nothing, and ate his fish.

One day when Mr Seeders came in for his meal, he drank too much beer. He finished his fish, got up, put his arm round Tildy, kissed her loudly, and walked out of the restaurant.

For a few seconds Tildy just stood there. Then Aileen said to her, 'Why, Tildy! You bad girl! I must watch you. I don't want to lose my men to you!'

Suddenly Tildy's world changed. She understood now that men could like her and want her as much as Aileen. She, Tildy, could have a love-life, too. Her eyes were bright, and her face was pink. She wanted to tell everybody her secret. When the restaurant was quiet, she went and stood by Bogle's desk.

'Do you know what a man in the restaurant did to me

today?' she said. 'He put his arm round me and he kissed me!'

'Really!' Bogle answered. This was good for business. 'Next week you'll get a dollar a week more.'

And when, in the evening, the restaurant was busy again, Tildy put down the food on the tables and said quietly, 'Do you know what a man in the restaurant did to me today? He put his arm round me and kissed me!'

Some of the men in the restaurant were surprised; some of them said, 'Well done!' Men began to smile and say nice things to her. Tildy was very happy. Love was now possible in her grey life.

For two days Mr Seeders did not come again, and in that time Tildy was a different woman. She wore bright clothes, did her hair differently, and she looked taller and thinner. Now she was a real woman because someone loved her. She felt excited, and a little afraid. What would Mr Seeders do the next time he came in?

At four o'clock in the afternoon of the third day, Mr Seeders came in. There were no people at the tables, and Aileen and Tildy were working at the back of the restaurant. Mr Seeders walked up to them.

Tildy looked at him, and she could not speak. Mr Seeders' face was very red, and he looked uncomfortable.

'Miss Tildy,' he said, 'I want to say that I'm sorry for what I did to you a few days ago. It was the drink, you see. I didn't know what I was doing. I'm very sorry.'

And Mr Seeders left.

But Tildy ran into the kitchen, and she began to cry. She

could not stop crying. She was no longer beautiful. No man loved her. No man wanted her. The kiss meant nothing to Mr Seeders. Tildy did not like him very much, but the kiss was important to her – and now there was nothing.

But she still had her friend, and Aileen put her arm round Tildy. Aileen did not really understand, but she said, 'Don't be unhappy, Tildy. That little Seeders has got a face like a dead potato! He's nothing. A real man never says sorry!'

WORD FOCUS

Perhaps Mr Seeders phoned a friend about his moment with Tildy. Complete their conversation with these words. (Use one word in each gap.)

arm, beautiful, beer, bright, different, fat, happy, kissed, mean, sorry, tall, terrible, waitresses, wrong

SEEDERS: Jeff, I need to talk to you. I've done something _____.

JEFF: Really? What did you do?

SEEDERS: Well, three days ago I was at Bogle's for lunch. Do you remember the two _____ there?

JEFF: I remember one of them – she's _____ and _____.

SEEDERS: Yes, that's Aileen. But I'm talking about Tildy.

JEFF: I don't remember her.

SEEDERS: No, nobody does. She's small and ____.

JEFF: Well, go on. What happened? What did you do?

SEEDERS: I drank too much _____. And at the end of my meal, I walked up to Tildy, put my _____ round her, and _____ her. Just like that! Don't laugh!

JEFF: I'm not laughing! But why did you kiss her? Do you love her?

SEEDERS: Of course not. The kiss didn't _____ anything. It was just because of the beer. But I went to Bogle's again today and Tildy looked different. She was wearing _____ clothes, her hair was _____ . . . and she looked very _____ to see me.

JEFF: That's nice.

SEEDERS: No, it's not! I told her I was _____ for kissing her, and then she ran away! Did I do the _____ thing? I don't understand.

JEFF: Okay. Now, listen to me . . .

Story Focus 1

What do you think about the people in this story? Choose some names from the list and complete these sentences in your own words.

Aileen / Tildy / Mr Seeders

1 I felt sorry for _____ because ________.
2 I thought _____ was right / wrong to ________.
3 I thought _____ did a good / bad thing when ________.
4 I liked it when ________.
5 I think _____ made a mistake when ________.

Story Focus 2

Here are four new endings for the story. Which do you prefer? Explain why, or write a new ending for the story yourself.

1 Two weeks later, Mr Seeders decides that he really loves Tildy. Soon they get married.
2 Now Tildy knows that men like her, she gets a job as an actress. Soon she is very famous.
3 Tildy runs from the restaurant and never returns. Nobody sees her at Bogle's again.
4 The next week, a young man comes in to Bogle's and kisses Tildy. Nobody knows why men are kissing her!

Andrew, Jane, the Parson, and the Fox

Some weddings are wonderful from beginning to end. Everything goes right, the sun shines, the bride is beautiful, nobody is late, and everybody is happy. But not every wedding is like that.

Jane needs to get married quickly, but Andrew is not really sure he wants to be a husband. And when they arrive at the church for the wedding, the parson is cross with them and wants to send them away again. It's a wedding full of mistakes and locked doors and things going wrong – and it was all because of the fox, of course . . .

THOMAS HARDY

Andrew, Jane, the Parson, and the Fox

Retold by Jennifer Bassett

It all happened because Andrew Satchel liked his drink too much. Jane Vallens, his bride, was some years older than him, and was in a great hurry to get married. Andrew agreed to marry her because of the baby, but he didn't really want to get married, and Jane, poor thing, was afraid of losing him. She was very anxious to get him to church as soon as possible.

So she was very happy, early on a fine November morning, when she and Andrew walked to the church just outside her village. Andrew's brother and sister went with them, to be their witnesses. After the wedding Andrew and Jane planned to go down to Port Bredy and spend the day there, as a little holiday.

When Andrew left Longpuddle that morning, to walk to his bride's village, people said that he was walking all over the road, first one side, then the other. The night before, you see, he was at his neighbour's house, for a party to welcome a new baby. It was a good party, and Andrew had no sleep, and a lot of strong drink.

He got to the church with Jane, they walked inside, and the parson looked at Andrew very hard.

'What's this? You're drunk, my man! And so early in the morning, too! That's disgraceful!'

'Well, that's true, sir,' said Andrew. 'But I can stand, and I can walk. Better than a lot of people. You couldn't stand and walk after a party at Tom Forrest's house, could you, Parson? No, you couldn't!'

This answer didn't please Parson Billy Toogood a bit. He was strong on church business inside the church, but he was very different outside the church, I can tell you.

'I cannot marry you when you are drunk, and I will not!' he said. 'Go home and get sober!'

Then the bride began to cry. 'Oh Parson, please marry us, please!'

'No, I won't,' said Mr Toogood. 'I won't marry you to a man who is drunk. It's not right. I'm sorry for you, young woman, because I can see that you need to get married, but you must go home. How could you bring him here drunk like this?'

'But if he doesn't come drunk, he won't come at all, sir!' said Jane, still crying hard.

But Parson Toogood still said no.

'Well, sir,' said Jane, 'please will you go home and leave us here for two hours? When you come back, Andrew will be sober. But I want to stay here, because if Andrew goes out of this church unmarried, wild horses won't get him back here again!'

'Very well,' said Parson Toogood. 'I'll give you two hours, and then I'll come back.'

Andrew's brother and sister didn't want to wait all that time, so the church clerk sent them home. 'We'll find some other people to be witnesses,' he said.

Then the bride whispered in the parson's ear. 'Please, sir, will you lock the door – and not tell anyone we are here? And perhaps it will be better if you put us in the church tower. If we stay here in the church, people can look in the windows and see us and talk about it. And perhaps Andrew will try to get out and leave me!'

'All right,' said the parson. 'We'll lock you in.'

Then he and the church clerk went home, the parson into his house, and the clerk into the garden. The clerk worked for the parson, you see – in the garden, taking care of his horses, and that kind of thing. And both of them, parson and clerk, dearly loved following the hunt.

Well, on that day the hunt was meeting near the parson's village, and soon both the parson and the clerk could hear the noise of the horses, and the dogs, and everything. The clerk hurried into the house.

'Sir,' he said. 'The hunt's here, and your horses need a run very badly, sir. They haven't been out for days!'

'You're right,' said Parson Toogood. 'Yes, the horses must go out. Go and get them ready! We'll take them out, just for an hour, and then come back.'

So the clerk got the horses ready, and he and the parson rode off to find the hunt. When they got there, the parson found a lot of friends, and soon they were all talking and laughing together. Then the dogs found a fox, and away they all went – the huntsmen in their red coats, the squire from the big house with his friends, the farmers and their sons, and the parson and the clerk.

He was a great hunting man, was Parson Toogood. He

forgot all about the unmarried man and woman locked in his church tower, and so did the clerk.

Across the fields they rode, over the hedges, through the rivers, in and out of woods, up and down the hills. It was a fine, exciting run that day, and the parson and the clerk enjoyed themselves very much. At one time the fox turned back, and ran right under the nose of Parson Toogood's horse.

'Halloo! Halloo!' shouted the parson. 'There he goes!' and away they all went again.

At last, late in the day, the hunt came to an end. The parson and the clerk were a long way from home, and their horses were tired. They rode home very slowly.

'Oh dear, my back does hurt!' said Parson Toogood.

'I can't keep my eyes open,' said the clerk. 'I'm so tired!'

It was dark when they got home. They made the horses comfortable, ate something, and fell into bed themselves.

The next morning, when Parson Toogood was having breakfast, the clerk came running in through the door.

'Oh sir!' he cried. 'Those two in the church tower – we forgot all about them! They'll still be there!'

Parson Toogood jumped up from his chair. 'Oh dear!' he said. 'Oh dear, oh dear! This is disgraceful!'

'It is, sir; very. And that poor woman . . .'

'Don't say it, clerk! If she's had the baby, and no doctor or nurse with her . . . Come on!'

So they both ran round to the church, looked up at the tower, and saw a little white face looking down at them. It was the bride.

'They're still there,' said the parson. He turned his face away. 'Oh dear, oh dear! What am I going to say to them? Is she all right, clerk? Can you see?'

'I don't know, sir. I can't see lower than her neck.'

'Well, how does her face look?'

'White, sir. Very, very white.'

'Well, we must go in and see them. Oh dear, oh dear! And my back still hurts from that ride yesterday!'

They went into the church and unlocked the tower door, and at once poor Jane and Andrew jumped out like hungry cats from a cupboard. Andrew was very sober now, and his bride was white in the face, but all right in other ways.

'Thank God for that!' said Parson Toogood. 'But why didn't you try to escape? Why didn't you shout from the top of the tower, to get help?'

'She didn't want me to,' said Andrew.

Jane began to cry again. 'It was the disgrace of it,' she said. 'We thought people would talk about it and laugh at us all our lives. So we waited and waited and waited – but you never came back, parson!'

'Yes, I'm sorry about that,' said Parson Toogood. 'Very sorry. But now, let's get on with the wedding.'

'I'd like something to eat first,' said Andrew. 'Just a piece of bread. I'm so hungry – I could eat a horse!'

'Oh, let's get married first,' said the bride anxiously, 'while the parson's still here. It won't take a minute.'

'Oh, all right,' said Andrew.

The clerk was one witness, and he called in a second

witness (telling him not to talk about it). Very soon Andrew and Jane were husband and wife.

'Now,' said Parson Toogood, 'you two must come back to my house and eat a good meal.'

So they went back with the parson, and ate nearly every bit of food in his house.

They kept the secret for a while, but then the story got out, and everybody knew about their night in the church tower. Even Andrew and Jane laugh about it now. Andrew isn't much of a husband, it's true, but Jane got a ring on her finger and a name for her baby.

WORD FOCUS

Match each word with an appropriate meaning. Then use nine of the words from the list to complete the passage below.

Words	Meanings
anxious	a wild animal like a dog, with a long tail and red fur
bride	a person who sees something happen and can say that it truly happened
clerk	not drunk
disgraceful	an old word for a priest in the church
drunk	a tall part of a building, for example, on a church
fox	when people ride horses and chase foxes with dogs
hunt *(n)*	the time when a man and a woman get married
neighbour	behaving differently after drinking too much alcohol
parson	a woman on the day of her wedding
sober	somebody who helps a parson in his work
tower	very bad; making people feel sorry and ashamed
wedding	a person who lives near you
witness	if you are ____ to do something, you want to do it very much

Here is someone telling the villagers a funny story. Who is speaking?

'. . . and when they got to the church, Andrew was still _____. The _____ said it was _____ and he wouldn't marry them. He told them to come back when Andrew was _____. But Jane was _____ to get married that day, so she asked the parson to lock them in the church _____. We did that and went home. But later we went out to join the _____ and we were out riding all day. We forgot all about the _____ and her young man in the church! And so the _____ didn't happen until the next day.'

Story Focus

Here are three short passages from the story. Read them and answer the questions.

> 'And so early in the morning, too. That's disgraceful.'

1 Who says these words in the story, and to whom?
2 Where is the speaker when he says this?
3 What does the speaker think is 'disgraceful'?

> 'I'm sorry for you, young woman, because I can see that you need to get married, but you must go home.'

4 Who says these words in the story, and to whom?
5 Why does the speaker say that the young woman 'needs' to get married?
6 Why must the young woman go home? Do you agree with the speaker?

> 'Oh dear, oh dear! This is disgraceful!'

7 Who is speaking, and to whom?
8 What does the speaker think is 'disgraceful'?
9 There are two 'disgraceful' things in these passages. Which is worse, do you think?

About the Authors

~

SAIT FAIK ABASIYANIK

Sait Faik (1906–1954) was born in Adapazari in Turkey. He went to school in Istanbul, and studied at universities in Istanbul, Switzerland, and France, where he lived for about three years. He returned to Turkey in 1935. He tried a number of different jobs – businessman, teacher, journalist – but he never stayed in any job for long. His first love was writing, and in 1936 he published his first volume of short stories, *The Samovar*. He never married, and for most of his life he lived with his mother in the family home on Burgaz Island, near Istanbul.

During his short life Sait Faik wrote two novels, many essays, forty poems, and more than 190 short stories. He is one of the greatest Turkish writers of short stories, and is often compared to the famous Russian writer Anton Chekhov. His stories are about ordinary people's lives – Armenian fishermen, Greek priests, office workers, waiters, children, criminals . . . He was interested in everybody – good, bad, poor, unhappy, unimportant. 'I love people more than flags,' he wrote. 'Everything starts with loving a person.'

In 1953 he was made an honorary member of the Mark Twain Association in the United States, and since 1955 the Sait Faik Short Story Award is given each year to the best collection of short stories.

YALVAC URAL

Yalvac Ural (1945–) was born in Konya in Turkey. He is a famous writer of children's books and has won many prizes in Turkey and abroad. He is also a poet, writing poetry mostly for children but also for adults. A musician as well as a writer, he has played in many bands, and a few years ago began playing the saxophone.

He works as a journalist and an editor, and during twenty-three years has published a wide range of children's magazines. He is a well-known contributor to children's programmes on Turkish television.

One of his children's books, *La Fontaine On Trial In The Forest (La Fonten Orman Mahkemesinde)*, has been published and illustrated many times, and is performed in almost every school theatre in Turkey.

In 1986 Yalvac Ural received the International Order of the Smile ('Orderu Usmiechu') from children in Poland, which recognized his ability to make the children of the world smile.

JENNIFER BASSETT

Jennifer Bassett has worked in English Language Teaching since 1972. She has been a teacher, teacher trainer, editor, and materials writer, and has taught students from all over the world. She now lives in Devon, in the south-west of England, and has been the Series Editor of the Oxford Bookworms Library for many years. She is also series co-adviser, with H. G. Widdowson, of the Oxford Bookworms Collection.

In twenty years of story-telling, she has written or edited more than two hundred stories for English language learners. For the Oxford Bookworms Library her original titles at Stage 1 and Stage 2 are *One-Way Ticket*, *The President's Murderer*, *The Phantom of the Opera*, *The Omega Files*, *William Shakespeare*, and she has retold for Bookworms many stories and novels from both classic and modern fiction. Her stories in this book, *Mr Harris and the Night Train* and *Omega File 349*, are from her Bookworms titles *One-Way Ticket* and *The Omega Files*.

Jennifer Bassett enjoys walking across the quiet Devon hills, swimming in warm tropical seas, and reading, writing, and thinking about stories.

JOHN ESCOTT

John Escott was born in Somerset in the west of England, but now lives in Bournemouth on the south coast. He began by writing books for children, but has written or retold more than a hundred graded readers for English language learners. He writes both fiction and non-fiction, but enjoys writing crime and mystery thrillers most of all.

His original stories for the Oxford Bookworms Library are *Girl on a Motorcycle* and *Star Reporter*, both at Starter Level. At Bookworms Stage 1 his titles are *Goodbye, Mr Hollywood* and *Sister Love and Other Crime Stories*. The story in this book, *Sister Love*, comes from that volume. His titles at Stage 2 are *Dead Man's Island* and *Agatha Christie, Woman of Mystery*, which is the true story of the life of perhaps the most famous mystery writer of all.

When he is not working, John Escott likes looking for long-forgotten books in small back-street bookshops or on the Internet. He also enjoys watching old Hollywood movies on video or DVD, and walking for miles along empty beaches on the south coast of England.

O. HENRY

O. Henry (1862–1910), whose real name was William Sydney Porter, was born in North Carolina in the USA. When he was twenty, he went to Texas and worked in many different offices and then in a bank. In 1887 he married a young woman called Athol Estes, and he and Athol were very happy together. His most famous short story is *The Gift of the Magi*, and many people think that Della in that story is based on his wife Athol.

In 1896 Porter ran away to Honduras because people said he stole money from the bank when he was working there in 1894. A year later he came back to Texas to see his wife Athol, who was dying, and in 1898 he was sent to prison. During his time there he published many short stories, and when he left prison in 1901, he was already a famous writer.

Porter's stories are both sad and funny, and show a great understanding of the everyday lives of ordinary people. He wrote about six hundred stories and made a lot of money, but he was a very unhappy man. When he died, he had only twenty-three cents in his pocket, and his last words were:

'Turn up the lights; I don't want to go home in the dark.'

THOMAS HARDY

Thomas Hardy (1840–1928) was born in a small village in Dorset, in the south of England. When he was a young man, he often played the fiddle at weddings and parties, and he loved listening to old people telling stories of country life. Later, Hardy put many of the characters and events from these stories into his own short stories and novels.

At twenty-two, he went to London to work as an architect, and there he started writing poems, stories, and novels. His fourth novel, *Far from the Madding Crowd*, was very popular, and from this he earned enough money to stop working and also to get married. He wrote several other successful novels, but some readers did not like them, saying they were dark and cruel. After this, Hardy stopped writing novels and returned to poetry.

For most of his life, he lived in Dorset with his first wife, Emma. Soon after she died, he married again. After his death his heart was buried in Emma's grave.

READING CIRCLE ROLES

When you work on your role sheet, remember these words:

~ READ ~ THINK ~ CONNECT ~ ASK ~~ AND CONNECT

READ ~

- Read the story once without stopping.
- Read it again while you work on your role sheet.

THINK ~

- Look for passages in the story that are interesting or unusual. Think about them. Prepare some questions to ask about them.
- Think about the meanings of words. If you use a dictionary, try to use an English-to-English learner's dictionary.

CONNECT ~

- Connect with the characters' thoughts and feelings. Perhaps it is a horror story and we cannot 'connect' with an experience like this, but we can see how the characters are thinking or feeling.

ASK ~

- Ask questions with many possible answers; questions that begin with *How? Why? What? Who?* Do not ask *yes/no* questions.
- When you ask questions, use English words that everyone in your circle can understand, so that everyone can talk about the story.

AND CONNECT ~

- Connect with your circle. Share your ideas, listen to other people's ideas. If you don't understand something, ask people to repeat or explain. And have fun!

The role sheets are on the next six pages (and on page 90 there are role badges you can make). Bigger role sheets, with space for writing, are in the Teacher's Handbook. Or you can read about your role in these pages, and write your notes and questions in your own notebook.

Discussion Leader

STORY: ______________________________

NAME: ______________________________

The Discussion Leader's job is to . . .

- read the story twice, and prepare at least five general questions about it.
- ask one or two questions to start the Reading Circle discussion.
- make sure that everyone has a chance to speak and joins in the discussion.
- call on each member to present their prepared role information.
- guide the discussion and keep it going.

Usually the best discussion questions come from your own thoughts, feelings, and questions as you read. (What surprised you, made you smile, made you feel sad?) Write down your questions as soon as you have finished reading. It is best to use your own questions, but you can also use some of the ideas at the bottom of this page.

MY QUESTIONS:

1 ______________________________

__ ______________________________

__ ______________________________

__ ______________________________

__ ______________________________

__ ______________________________

__ ______________________________

__ ______________________________

Other general ideas:

- Questions about the characters (*like / not like them, true to life / not true to life ...?*)
- Questions about the theme (*friendship, romance, parents/children, ghosts ...?*)
- Questions about the ending (*surprising, expected, liked it / did not like it ...?*)
- Questions about what will happen next. (These can also be used for a longer story.)

Summarizer

STORY: ______________________

NAME: ______________________

The Summarizer's job is to . . .

- read the story and make notes about the characters, events, and ideas.
- find the key points that everyone must know to understand and remember the story.
- retell the story in a short summary (one or two minutes) in your own words.
- talk about your summary to the group, using your writing to help you.

Your reading circle will find your summary very useful, because it will help to remind them of the plot and the characters in the story. You may need to read the story more than once to make a good summary, and you may need to repeat it to the group a second time.

MY KEY POINTS:

Main events:
Characters:

MY SUMMARY:

Connector

STORY: ____________________

NAME: ____________________

The Connector's job is to . . .

- read the story twice, and look for connections between the story and the world outside.
- make notes about at least two possible connections to your own experiences, or to the experiences of friends and family, or to real-life events.
- tell the group about the connections and ask for their comments or questions.
- ask the group if they can think of any connections themselves.

These questions will help you think about connections while you are reading.
Events: Has anything similar ever happened to you, or to someone you know? Does anything in the story remind you of events in the real world? For example, events you have read about in newspapers, or heard about on television news programmes.
Characters: Do any of them remind you of people you know? How? Why? Have you ever had the same thoughts or feelings as these characters have? Do you know anybody who thinks, feels, behaves like that?

MY CONNECTIONS:

Word Master

STORY: ____________________

NAME: ____________________

The Word Master's job is to . . .

- read the story, and look for words or short phrases that are new or difficult to understand, or that are important in the story.
- choose five words (only five) that you think are important for this story.
- explain the meanings of these five words in simple English to the group.
- tell the group why these words are important for understanding this story.

Your five words do not have to be new or unknown words. Look for words in the story that really stand out in some way. These may be words that are:

- repeated often
- used in an unusual way
- important to the meaning of the story

MY WORDS	MEANING OF THE WORD	REASON FOR CHOOSING THE WORD
______ PAGE ______ LINE ______		
______ PAGE ______ LINE ______		
______ PAGE ______ LINE ______		
______ PAGE ______ LINE ______		
______ PAGE ______ LINE ______		

Passage Person

STORY: ______________________________

NAME: ______________________________

The Passage Person's job is to . . .

- read the story, and find important, interesting, or difficult passages.
- make notes about at least three passages that are important for the plot, or that explain the characters, or that have very interesting or powerful language.
- read each passage to the group, or ask another group member to read it.
- ask the group one or two questions about each passage.

A passage is usually one paragraph, but sometimes it can be just one or two sentences, or perhaps a piece of dialogue. You might choose a passage to discuss because it is:

• important • informative • surprising • funny • confusing • well-written

MY PASSAGES:

PAGE ________ **LINES** ________

REASONS FOR CHOOSING THE PASSAGE	QUESTIONS ABOUT THE PASSAGE

PAGE ________ **LINES** ________

REASONS FOR CHOOSING THE PASSAGE	QUESTIONS ABOUT THE PASSAGE

PAGE ________ **LINES** ________

REASONS FOR CHOOSING THE PASSAGE	QUESTIONS ABOUT THE PASSAGE

Culture Collector

STORY: ______________________

NAME: ______________________

The Culture Collector's job is to . . .

- read the story, and look for both differences and similarities between your own culture and the culture found in the story.
- make notes about two or three passages that show these cultural points.
- read each passage to the group, or ask another group member to read it.
- ask the group some questions about these, and any other cultural points in the story.

Here are some questions to help you think about cultural differences.
Theme: What is the theme of this story (for example, getting married, meeting a ghost, murder, unhappy children)? Is this an important theme in your own culture? Do people think about this theme in the same way, or differently?
People: Do characters in this story say or do things that people never say or do in your culture? Do they say or do some things that everybody in the world says or does?

MY CULTURAL COLLECTION (differences and similarities):

1 **PAGE** ________ **LINES** ________ : ______________________

____

2 **PAGE** ________ **LINES** ________ : ______________________

____

MY CULTURAL QUESTIONS:

1 ______________________

— ______________________

— ______________________

— ______________________

PLOT PYRAMID ACTIVITY

A **plot** is a series of events which form a story. The Reading Circles **Plot Pyramid** is a way of looking at and talking about the plot of a story. The pyramid divides the story into five parts.

The Exposition gives the background needed to understand the story. It tells us who the characters are, where the story happens, and when it happens. Sometimes we also get an idea about problems to come.

The Complication is the single event which begins the conflict, or creates the problem. The event might be an action, a thought, or words spoken by one of the characters.

The Rising Action brings more events and difficulties. As the story moves through these events, it gets more exciting, and begins to take us toward the climax.

The Climax is the high point of the story, the turning point, the point of no return. It marks a change, for better or for worse, in the lives of one or more of the characters.

The Resolution usually offers an answer to the problem or the conflict, which may be sad or happy for the characters. Mysteries are explained, secrets told, and the reader can feel calm again.

HOW TO PLOT THE PYRAMID

1. Read your story again, and look for each part of the pyramid as you read. Make notes, or mark your book.
2. In your Reading Circle, find each part of the pyramid in the story, and then write down your ideas. Use the boxes in the diagram opposite as a guide (a bigger diagram, with space for writing in the boxes, is in the Teacher's Handbook).
3. Begin with the *Exposition*, and work through the *Complication*, the *Rising Action* (only two points), the *Climax*, and the *Resolution*.
4. Finally, your group draws the pyramid and writes the notes on the board, and then presents the pyramid to the class.

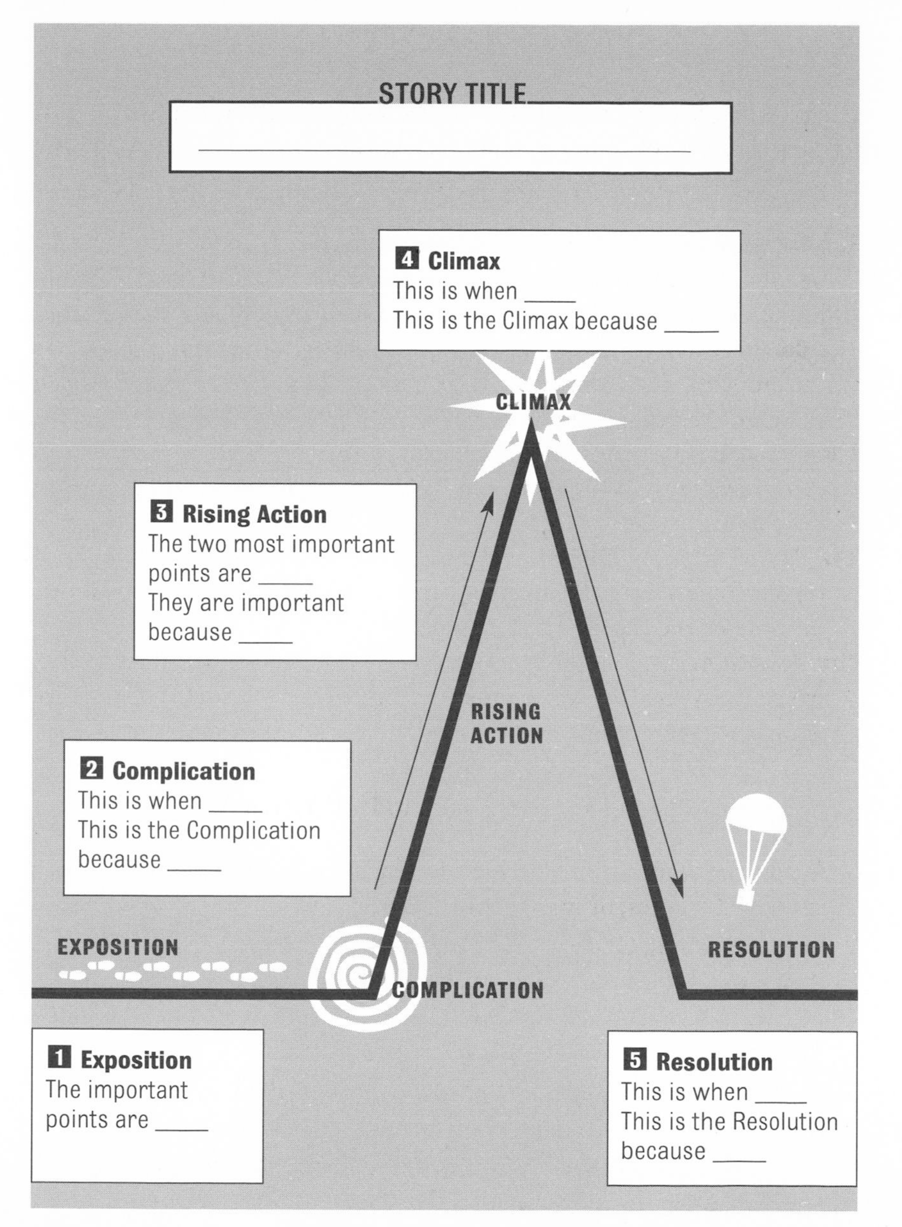
STORY TITLE
4 Climax
This is when ____
This is the Climax because ____
CLIMAX
3 Rising Action
The two most important points are ____
They are important because ____
RISING ACTION
2 Complication
This is when ____
This is the Complication because ____
EXPOSITION
COMPLICATION
RESOLUTION
1 Exposition
The important points are ____
5 Resolution
This is when ____
This is the Resolution because ____

POSTER ACTIVITY

Each Reading Circle group makes a poster in English about a story in this book. Posters can have words, pictures, and drawings. Your group will need to find extra information about the story – perhaps from the Internet, or the school library, or your teacher.

Use the ideas on the opposite page to help you. When all the posters are finished, each Reading Circle will present their own poster to the other groups. At the end, keep all the posters, and make a 'poster library'.

THE THEME

What is the theme of the story?

- Is it about love or murder or friendship? Is it about dreams or wishes or fears?

THE TIME, THE PLACE

What do you know about the time and the place of the story?

- the city / the country?
- a real world, or an unreal world?
- If the time and place are not given, does it matter?

THE WRITER

What interesting facts do you know about the author's life?

- Was he or she also a poet, an actor, a teacher? Or a spy, a sailor, a thief, a doctor, a madman?

THE BACKGROUND

What cultural information did you learn from the story?

- About family events (for example, a wedding)
- A national holiday
- Family life (for example, parents and children)

THE LANGUAGE

What did you like about the language in the story?

- Find a quotation you like – words that are funny or clever or sad, or words that paint a picture in your mind.

THE FILM

Direct your own film! Who will play the characters in the film?

- Choose the best actors to play the characters.
- Where will you film it?
- Will you change the story?
- What title will the film have?

BOOKWORMS CLUB SILVER
Stories for Reading Circles
STAGES 2 AND 3

Editor: Mark Furr

In these seven short stories we find all kinds of people – a young couple in love, a clever young woman, a boy with an unhappy father, a madman, a famous detective, a daughter who stays out late, a man who cannot remember who he is . . .

The Bookworms Club brings together a selection of adapted short stories from other Bookworms titles. These stories have been specially chosen for use with Reading Circles.

The Christmas Presents
O. Henry, from *New Yorkers*

Netty Sargent and the House
Thomas Hardy, from *Tales from Longpuddle*

Too Old to Rock and Roll
Jan Mark, from *Too Old to Rock and Roll and Other Stories*

A Walk in Amnesia
O. Henry, from *New Yorkers*

The Five Orange Pips
Sir Arthur Conan Doyle, from *Sherlock Holmes Short Stories*

The Tell-Tale Heart
Edgar Allan Poe, from *Tales of Mystery and Imagination*

Go, Lovely Rose
H. E. Bates, from *Go, Lovely Rose and Other Stories*

BOOKWORMS CLUB GOLD

Stories for Reading Circles

STAGES 3 AND 4

Editor: Mark Furr

In these seven short stories there are many different answers to life's little problems. How to plan the perfect murder – and succeed. How to choose – and keep – the perfect wife or husband. How to find hidden gold. How to live for two hundred years . . .

The Bookworms Club brings together a selection of adapted short stories from other Bookworms titles. These stories have been specially chosen for use with Reading Circles.

The Black Cat
Edgar Allan Poe, from *Tales of Mystery and Imagination*

Sredni Vashtar
Saki, from *Tooth and Claw*

The Railway Crossing
Freeman Wills Crofts, from *As the Inspector Said and Other Stories*

The Daffodil Sky
H. E. Bates, from *Go, Lovely Rose and Other Stories*

A Moment of Madness
Thomas Hardy, from *The Three Strangers and Other Stories*

The Secret
Arthur C. Clarke, from *The Songs of Distant Earth and Other Stories*

The Experiment
M. R. James, from *The Unquiet Grave*

ROLE BADGES

These role icons can be photocopied and then cut out to make badges or stickers for the members of the Reading Circle to wear.